FOCUS ON ENDANGERED SPECIES
ENDANGERED INSECTS

by Christa Kelly

BrightPoint Press

San Diego, CA

© 2024 BrightPoint Press
an imprint of ReferencePoint Press, Inc.
Printed in the United States

For more information, contact:
BrightPoint Press
PO Box 27779
San Diego, CA 92198
www.BrightPointPress.com

ALL RIGHTS RESERVED.

No part of this work covered by the copyright hereon may be reproduced or used in any form or by any means—graphic, electronic, or mechanical, including photocopying, recording, taping, web distribution, or information storage retrieval systems—without the written permission of the publisher.

LIBRARY OF CONGRESS CATALOGING-IN-PUBLICATION DATA

Names: Kelly, Christa, author.
Title: Endangered insects / by Christa Kelly.
Description: San Diego, CA: BrightPoint Press, [2024] | Series: Focus on endangered species | Includes bibliographical references and index. | Audience: Ages 13 | Audience: Grades 7-9
Identifiers: LCCN 2023009839 (print) | LCCN 2023009840 (eBook) | ISBN 9781678206444 (hardcover) | ISBN 9781678206451 (eBook)
Subjects: LCSH: Endangered insects--Juvenile literature. | Insects--Conservation--Juvenile literature. | Endangered invertebrates--Juvenile literature.
Classification: LCC QL467.8 .K45 2024 (print) | LCC QL467.8 (eBook) | DDC 595.7168--dc23/eng/20230323
LC record available at https://lccn.loc.gov/2023009839
LC eBook record available at https://lccn.loc.gov/2023009840

CONTENTS

AT A GLANCE	4
INTRODUCTION CONCRETE PRAIRIES	6
CHAPTER ONE MONARCH BUTTERFLIES	10
CHAPTER TWO HINE'S EMERALD DRAGONFLIES	20
CHAPTER THREE RUSTY PATCHED BUMBLE BEES	32
CHAPTER FOUR LORD HOWE ISLAND STICK INSECTS	46
Glossary	58
Source Notes	59
For Further Research	60
Index	62
Image Credits	63
About the Author	64

AT A GLANCE

- There are about 1 million known species of insects. Many of them are endangered due to human activity.

- Monarch butterflies live throughout the United States and southern parts of Canada. They are threatened by habitat loss.

- Some organizations are working to end the deforestation of monarch butterfly habitats. Others plant new trees where the butterflies hibernate.

- Scientists once thought Hine's emerald dragonflies were extinct, but some can still be found in wetlands in the United States.

- The University of South Dakota is raising Hine's emerald dragonflies in captivity. This increases their chances of survival.

- Rusty patched bumble bees are threatened by climate change. False springs can lead to queens coming out of hibernation too early and freezing.

- Conservationists encourage people to grow pollinator-friendly plants to help feed bees.

- Lord Howe Island stick insects were nearly driven to extinction after black rats invaded their island in the early 1900s. The rats ate all of the insects on Lord Howe Island, leading scientists to believe the species was extinct.

- In 2001, scientists discovered a small group of Lord Howe Island stick insects living on an island 12 miles (19 km) away. They took four of the insects and bred them in captivity. Conservationists are now working to reintroduce the bugs to their original habitat.

INTRODUCTION

CONCRETE PRAIRIES

A rusty patched bumble bee is looking for food. She's a worker bee. Her job is to collect nectar and pollen for her colony. But she hasn't found any food all day. Her huge compound eyes scan the landscape. All she sees are big grass lawns and concrete sidewalks.

This land used to be full of wildflowers and prairie grasses. Now the open fields are gone. Humans replaced the native plants with roads and houses. They left nothing for her colony to eat and almost nowhere for them to live.

The bee is getting tired. She needs food to keep flying. Suddenly she sees

Bumble bees visit up to 6,000 flowers every day.

something glowing. It's a dandelion. A human wouldn't be able to see the glow. But the bee's compound eyes can see ultraviolet light. The dandelion is growing from a crack in the sidewalk. The bee flies toward it.

The bee lands on the dandelion and sips up its nectar. When she's finished, she takes the dandelion in her jaws and beats her wings. This shakes the pollen loose. The bee's tiny hairs are now covered in bright-yellow pollen. The bee flies back toward her nest. She won't starve today. But how much longer can her colony last?

In 2019, about one-third of insect species were endangered.

ENDANGERED INSECTS

There are about 1 million known species of insects in the world. Many of these species are in danger. Some are threatened by **habitat** loss. Others are affected by climate change and pollution. By learning about endangered insects, people can learn how to protect these small species.

1
MONARCH BUTTERFLIES

Monarch butterflies are found throughout the United States and parts of southern Canada. They're best known for their two pairs of bright orange wings. Their wings are crossed with black veins. The edges are outlined with black and speckled with white spots. Their wings are made of thousands of tiny scales. The scales on the butterflies' midsections are long. This makes them look fuzzy.

Monarch butterflies have two antennae on the tops of their heads. They use their antennae to smell, stay balanced, detect motion, navigate, and tell time. Their sense

Monarch butterflies breathe through tiny holes in their bodies called spiracles.

of smell helps them find butterflies to mate with and food to eat.

Monarchs have compound eyes. These work like thousands of little eyes put together. This lets them see above, below, behind, and in front of them all at once. Their eyes also let them see ultraviolet light. Many plants and butterflies have markings that can be seen only in ultraviolet light.

Monarchs eat using a proboscis. This long organ acts as a straw to suck up nectar, fruit juices, water, and other liquids. The proboscis curls up under the butterfly's head when the butterfly isn't using it.

THE JOURNEY OF A MONARCH

Monarch butterflies spend their summers in Canada and the United States. But they can't survive cold winters. They have to find somewhere warmer to go. Every fall, monarchs travel up to 2,800 miles (4,500 km). Most travel to central Mexico.

POISONOUS BUTTERFLIES

Monarch caterpillars are poisonous to most predators. Monarch caterpillars eat milkweed. Milkweed is toxic to most creatures. The caterpillars' diet makes them toxic too. The insects are still poisonous as adults. The butterflies' bright colors warn predators that eating the insects will make the predators sick. This keeps the butterflies safe.

Others travel to the coast of California. This long journey is called a migration.

Most monarch butterflies live for only 2 to 6 weeks. But the last monarchs born before fall will live for 8 to 9 months. They have to survive long enough to complete their migration.

These tiny insects travel a long way. Scientists believe that monarchs have a natural compass in their brains. They've also **evolved** to use the Sun to find their way.

When the monarch butterflies arrive in Mexico, they huddle together on oyamel fir trees. Each tree can have tens of thousands

During the winter, trees in Mexico can be completely covered in monarch butterflies.

of monarchs on it. They'll **hibernate** there until the middle of March. Once the weather warms, the monarchs find a mate. Then they start the long journey back north to lay their eggs on milkweed plants.

BUTTERFLIES IN TROUBLE

These brilliant butterflies may not be around for much longer. Monarch populations shrank by up to 72 percent between 2012 and 2022. Human activity has made it much harder for them to survive.

One of the biggest dangers monarchs are facing is deforestation. Deforestation is when plants are cleared to make room for buildings. Much of the butterflies' habitat has been destroyed in Mexico. This means they don't have as much room to hibernate.

Monarch habitats up north are being destroyed too. People use poisons called herbicides to get rid of weeds. But these poisons can kill butterflies. Herbicides also kill milkweed. Monarch butterflies need milkweed. They lay their eggs on these plants. It's the only food that monarch caterpillars eat. Herbicides also kill other plants that make nectar. This takes away monarchs' food.

BACKING THE BUTTERFLIES

Conservationists are working hard to protect monarchs. Some grow

BEAUTIFUL CHANGES

After about 2 to 3 weeks of growing, a caterpillar will make a hard layer of skin around itself called a chrysalis. Its body breaks down inside the chrysalis. It then reforms. After about 10 days, an adult butterfly hatches from the chrysalis.

Planting pollinator-friendly plants, such as milkweed, is one way to support monarch butterflies.

pollinator-friendly plants in butterfly habitats. These plants have lots of nectar. Other conservationists teach people about the dangers of herbicides.

Habitat protection is also important. The World Wildlife Fund is working with people in Mexico to end the deforestation of monarch habitats. Other organizations are planting more oyamel fir trees. Forests for Monarchs is one such organization. By 2022, it had planted 11 million new trees.

Anna Walker studies endangered insects. She says, "It is difficult to watch monarch butterflies and their extraordinary migration teeter on the edge of collapse, but there are signs of hope. So many people and organizations have come together to try and protect this butterfly and its habitats. . . . We all have a role to play in making sure this iconic insect makes a full recovery."[1]

2
HINE'S EMERALD DRAGONFLIES

Hine's emerald dragonflies have slim, shiny bodies. They can be green, brown, or black. These dragonflies have a wingspan of about 3.5 inches (8.9 cm). They have two pairs of wings. The dragonflies' wings are mostly clear and checkered with yellow-brown veins. The dragonflies have huge green eyes. They can also be identified by the two yellow stripes along their sides.

THE LIFE OF A DRAGONFLY

Hine's emerald dragonflies begin their lives as eggs. They hatch into larvae.

Dragonflies are fast predators. They can fly at 35 miles per hour (56 kmh).

The larvae live in shallow water for about 2 to 4 years. They spend their time hunting and growing. When they're mature, they crawl out of the water. They inflate their bodies with air and expand into adult dragonflies.

Adult dragonflies live for only about 5 to 6 weeks. They spend their lives mating and hunting. They eat mosquitoes, flies, gnats, and other flying bugs.

DRAGONFLIES IN DANGER

The Hine's emerald dragonfly was discovered in 1929 by a scientist named

James S. Hine. Habitat loss caused it to disappear. By the mid-1900s, the population had shrunk so much that scientists believed the Hine's emerald dragonfly was extinct. But in 1987, the dragonfly was rediscovered in Wisconsin.

Hine's emerald dragonflies are threatened by habitat loss. They can live only

FRIENDS WITH FOES

Hine's emerald dragonfly larvae depend on devil crayfish to survive. The larvae live in crayfish dens during dry periods. This keeps them from drying out. Sometimes the larvae can stay unnoticed. Other times the crayfish find them and eat them.

in **wetlands**. But many wetlands are being drained to make room for buildings.

Pollution is another danger for the dragonflies. Farmers often use poisons designed to kill bugs to protect their plants. These poisons are called pesticides. Rain can wash pesticides into dragonfly habitats. This pollution can kill insects. Pesticides can also make it hard for dragonflies to have babies.

Invasive plants are another threat facing Hine's emerald dragonflies. Invasive plants are plants that aren't natural to a given habitat. Many are brought to new

Hine's emerald dragonfly larvae look very different from adult dragonflies. They are covered in rough hairs and use gills to breathe underwater.

habitats by humans. Some are brought accidentally. The European common reed is an invasive plant. It's taking over Hine's emerald dragonfly habitats. It steals nutrients from the wetlands. Its roots release a toxin that kills native plants. The loss of native plants can kill species that dragonfly larvae depend on. The plant also sucks up wetlands' water. The loss of water can kill dragonfly larvae.

These threats have hurt Hine's emerald dragonfly populations. They used to be found in seven midwestern states. By 2023, they remained in only four.

SAVING THE DRAGONFLIES

The University of South Dakota (USD) is working to raise Hine's emerald dragonfly populations. Researchers at the school visit dragonfly habitats. They capture female dragonflies and take their eggs. The adult dragonflies are released. The eggs are taken back to a laboratory. They're raised there for about 4 to 5 years. Mature dragonflies are released into the wild. Raising the insects in captivity increases the number of dragonflies that survive to adulthood.

ANCIENT RELATIVES

Dragonflies have been around for more than 300 million years. They existed before dinosaurs. Ancient dragonflies used to be a lot bigger than dragonflies are today. The largest known dragonfly had a wingspan of about 2.5 feet (76 cm). It weighed more than 1 pound (450 g). That's as big as a crow.

In 2020, ecologist Andres Ortega worked with the Hine's emerald dragonfly research program at USD. He explains why saving the dragonfly is so important. "Every species of plant or animal plays a role in the food chain even if we don't know what it is," he says. "And we don't want to find out the hard way." He adds, "Extinctions happen all the time. It's a natural process, but when we humans cause it we have an obligation to step in and try to correct it."[2]

The Center for Biological Diversity is another organization that's fighting for these endangered dragonflies. In 1995,

Cars are among the threats facing Hine's emerald dragonflies. About 3,300 are killed in vehicle collisions every year.

Hine's emerald dragonflies were added to the federal list of endangered species. This was an important step. Being on the US endangered species list gives animals protections. It makes it illegal for

29

them to be hurt or killed. It also protects their habitats. However, the US Fish and Wildlife Service (USFWS) didn't protect the dragonfly's habitats. In 2004, the Center for Biological Diversity sued the USFWS. The center demanded the dragonfly habitats be protected. After 6 years of court cases, the center won. The Hine's emerald dragonfly was given more than 26,500 acres (10,700 ha) of protected land.

John Buse is an attorney with the Center for Biological Diversity. He explains how important this win was. He says, "Thanks to the designation, Hine's emerald

USFWS rangers put some Hine's emerald dragonfly larvae in special cages during the winter to keep the larvae safe. Air pumped near the cages keeps the larvae's pond water from freezing.

dragonflies now have a chance to recover from the brink of extinction. Protecting habitat is the best way to bring back these spectacular insect predators."[3]

3
RUSTY PATCHED BUMBLE BEES

Rusty patched bumble bees can be hard to tell apart from other bumble bees. Like other bumble bees, they're round and fuzzy. They have two pairs of mostly clear wings lined with brown veins. They have black heads, black lower abdomens, and striped black and yellow midsections.

Most rusty patched bumble bees have a small patch of darker hair on their lower midsections. The color can range from brown to orange. They also have

Rusty patched bumble bees have short tongues. This means they can eat only from flowers with easily accessible nectar.

a T-shaped patch of black hair between their wings. The queen bees are the only members of the species that do not have the T-shape or the rusty patch. Queen bees are also bigger.

QUEEN OF THE COLONY

Rusty patched bumble bees are found in the eastern and upper midwestern United States and southern Canada. They live in groups called colonies. Colonies can have anywhere from fifty to 1,000 bees.

The rusty patched bumble bee queen hibernates underground during the winter.

She wakes up in the spring. Her first job is to find a place to live. She normally chooses an existing space, such as a rodent hole. The queen lines it with plant matter to make a nest. She then lays eggs. It takes about 3 days for the eggs to hatch. The eggs hatch into female worker bees. They become part of the queen's colony.

EYES EVERYWHERE

Rusty patched bumble bees have five eyes. Two are large compound eyes. The other three are called ocelli. These eyes are small. They're positioned in a triangle shape on the tops of the bees' heads. Ocelli can't see shapes. They can only sense light.

Worker bees collect food for the colony. Rusty patched bumble bees eat pollen and nectar. Worker bees get these foods from flowers. The worker bees are also responsible for taking care of young bees and protecting the colony.

The queen lays more eggs in late summer. These eggs are a mix of female and male. The new females will grow up to be queens. The males will mate with queens from other colonies. In the fall, all bees except for the new queens will die. The queens will hibernate and start their own colonies in the spring.

Scientists estimate that more than 40 percent of bee species worldwide are in danger of extinction.

THREATS TO THE RUSTY PATCHED BUMBLE BEE

The rusty patched bumble bee was once common across much of the eastern United States. Now it's facing extinction.

Habitat loss is one of its greatest threats. Since the 1990s, the bees' **range** has declined by 90 percent. Human activity is one of the biggest reasons for this habitat loss. Bees need lots of flowering plants to feed their colonies. When humans clear land for buildings and farms, the bees' habitats and food sources are cleared too.

Global warming also threatens the bees' food. When humans put pollutants such as **carbon dioxide** into the air, the gas traps heat from the sun. This makes the world hotter. Scientists call this global warming. Global warming can make droughts and

SHRINKING SPECIES

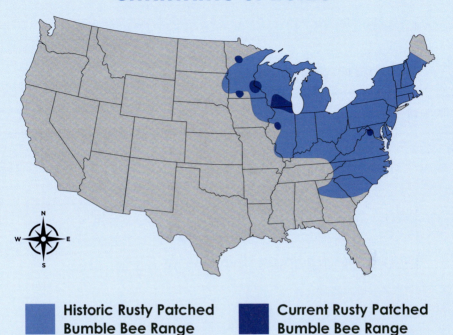

Rusty patched bumble bees used to live across the eastern United States. By the 2020s, their range had shrunk to a fraction of what it used to be.

fires more frequent. These disasters kill bees and their food sources.

Global warming can also cause bees to starve. Flowers can bloom early when winters are too warm. This is bad for queen bees. The flowers may be done blooming when the bees wake up. This leaves the queens with no food.

Warm winter weather can also make bees come out of hibernation too early. When the temperature drops again, they freeze to death. These factors have all led to a loss of bees. Since the 1990s, the rusty patched bumble bee's population has declined by 90 percent.

A WORLD WITHOUT POLLINATORS

This loss isn't just bad for the bees. Bees are pollinators. This means they carry pollen

Disease is a serious danger facing rusty patched bumble bees. Commercially farmed bees can transfer diseases to wild bee colonies.

between plants. This helps the plants make

seeds. Pollinators are needed to make

new plants.

Rusty patched bumble bees are powerful pollinators. They can buzz pollinate. This means they vibrate their wings to free pollen stuck in the plants. Some plants need this kind of pollination to grow.

Pati Vitt is the director of natural resources at Lake County Forest Preserves in Illinois. She explains why rusty patched bumble bees are so important. "They are a '**keystone species**' in functioning ecosystems," Vitt says. "Their work is necessary for wildflowers to reproduce and to create seeds and fruits that feed wildlife and humans."[4]

Bumble bees are among the only insects that can pollinate tomato plants.

BRINGING BACK THE BEES

Much of the work conservationists are doing to protect the rusty patched bumble bee involves education. They share ways for the public to support bees. One way to help bees is to grow pollinator-friendly plants.

These are plants that have a lot of pollen and nectar. They include lavender, bee balm, sunflowers, and more. Conservationists also teach people about the dangers of pesticides. Pesticides can kill bumble bees. Plants that are grown without pesticides provide bees with safer habitats.

Some conservationists teach people how to protect hibernating bees. They encourage people with lawns to avoid raking or gardening until summer. This gives queen bees living underground plenty of time to move to a new home. Other conservationists take it a step further.

It's important to grow bee-friendly plants. When more pollen is available, rusty patched bumble bees produce more queens.

They advocate for people to completely get rid of lawns. They say people should plant native plants instead of grass. This gives bees more food. It also gives them more places to live.

4
LORD HOWE ISLAND STICK INSECTS

The Lord Howe Island stick insect is huge. Some people call it a land lobster because of how big it is. It can grow up to 8 inches (20 cm) long. It can weigh up to 0.88 ounces (25 g). It has compound eyes and two long, thick antennae. A young Lord Howe Island stick insect is green. Its color changes to brown-black as it ages. Its body is glossy and **segmented**.

This huge insect can't fly. Instead, it relies on its speed to escape from predators. The Lord Howe Island stick insect can run very fast. It's also nimble. It can climb upside down.

Stick insects are also called phasmids. The Lord Howe Island stick insect may be the rarest phasmid in the world.

Young Lord Howe Island stick insects disguise themselves as leaves. They hang off branches and let their bodies shake in the wind to make their camouflage more convincing.

The Lord Howe Island stick insect was named after its habitat. Lord Howe Island is a tiny island off the eastern coast of Australia. Only a few hundred people live on the island, with 70 percent of the land protected as a nature reserve. While the island is home to many insects, the Lord Howe Island stick insect is no longer one of them.

LIFE AS A LORD HOWE

Lord Howe Island stick insects have a life span of about 1 to 1.5 years. They begin their lives as eggs. The young that hatch from the eggs are called nymphs. Nymphs are about 0.8 inches (2 cm) long. That's about three times the size of their eggs. Paige Howorth studies insects at the San Diego Zoo. She says that the nymphs are "folded up in [the eggs] like an origami piece."[5]

Lord Howe Island stick insect nymphs are active during the day. Their behavior changes as they get older. Adults are active only at night. They hide together during the day in plants and holes in trees and rocks.

Adult Lord Howe Island stick insects spend their evenings foraging for food. They eat only one type of plant in the wild. This plant is a species of shrub called melaleuca.

Lord Howe Island stick insects can have babies at about 6 months old. Some have babies **asexually**. Others find mates. Mates can form close bonds.

ON THE EDGE OF EXTINCTION

The Lord Howe stick insect used to be common on Lord Howe Island. In the early 1900s, there were enough that the species was regularly used as fishing bait. This changed in 1918. A ship called the

DEADLY FLOWERS

Rats aren't the only invasive species threatening the Lord Howe Island stick insects. Invasive plant species, such as morning glory flowers, are killing the shrubs that the insects eat. Scientists have gotten rid of the morning glory flowers from most of the bug's current habitat.

SS *Makambo* crashed on the island. Black rats had been hiding on the ship. They started living on the island. They ate many of the native species. This included the Lord Howe Island stick insect. They drove twenty of the island's native species to extinction. This included thirteen species of insects. By the early 1930s, the Lord Howe Island stick insect was thought to be extinct too.

About 12 miles (19 km) away from Lord Howe Island sits a small island called Ball's Pyramid. The island looks like a crumbling mountain reaching out of the sea. For the next 70 years, there were rumors that big

Geologists believe that Ball's Pyramid rose out of the ocean about 7 million years ago. The island is all that's left of an ancient volcano.

insects were living on the island. Some people said they had seen shed insect skin there. A few thought that the insect living there might be the Lord Howe Island stick insect.

In 2001, five scientists went to the island to investigate the rumors. They spent a day searching the island but found nothing. As they were about to leave the island, they found insect poop. It was clear that the insect that left it had been big. They waited until night. They knew that was when the insects would be the most active. Later that evening, two of the scientists found a melaleuca shrub. Hanging from the shrub were three Lord Howe Island stick insects.

BACK FROM THE DEAD

Conservationists started making plans for how to protect the rare insects. In 2003, scientists returned to the island.

They captured two breeding pairs of the stick insects. Scientists used the pairs to start a captive breeding program. By 2018, more than 14,000 Lord Howe Island stick insects had been bred.

The conservationists wanted to restore the insects to their natural habitat. But they first needed to get rid of the rats. Scientists estimated that there were 210,000 rats on

ADAM AND EVE

One of the two breeding pairs that scientists collected was given to Zoos Victoria in Australia. The zoo named the insects Adam and Eve. Eve laid 248 eggs. Most of the Lord Howe Island stick insects alive today are descended from this pair.

Lord Howe Island. Conservationists set out poisons, tracked the rats with cameras, and used rat-sniffing dogs to find and kill the invasive rodents. The project has been successful. As of 2022, no known rats were on the island.

 Scientists are also working to restore the Lord Howe Island stick insects' habitat. They're growing melaleuca shrubs and other native plants. These will provide the insects with food and shelter. Conservationists plan to release Lord Howe Island stick insects back into their original habitat.

Conservationists work to educate the public about Lord Howe Island stick insects. This helps people learn how to protect these rare insects.

Insects today are facing many threats. But they have many people fighting for them. By educating people and protecting insect habitats and resources, people around the world can save these small species.

GLOSSARY

asexually

without a mate

carbon dioxide

a gas that is created by burning fossil fuels such as oil and coal

evolved

changed over generations to adapt to an environment

habitat

where a species lives

hibernate

to slow down a body's functions to save energy, typically during winter

keystone species

a species that is necessary for an ecosystem's survival

range

the area in which a species can be found

segmented

divided into different parts

wetlands

places where the ground is full of water, such as swamps

SOURCE NOTES

CHAPTER ONE: MONARCH BUTTERFLIES

1. Quoted in "Migratory Monarch Butterfly Now Endangered—IUCN Red List," *IUCN*, July 21, 2022. www.iucn.org.

CHAPTER TWO: HINE'S EMERALD DRAGONFLIES

2. Quoted in Jack Murray, "Endangered Dragonfly Larvae from South Dakota Released into Lockport Prairie," *Chicago Tribune*, June 23, 2020. www.chicagotribune.com.

3. Quoted in "Habitat Doubled for Rare Dragonfly," *Center for Biological Diversity*, April 28, 2010. www.biologicaldiversity.org.

CHAPTER THREE: RUSTY PATCHED BUMBLE BEES

4. Quoted in "Rusty Patched Bumble Bee Sightings Increase in Lake County," *Lake County Forest Preserves*, September 21, 2022. www.lcfpd.org.

CHAPTER FOUR: LORD HOWE ISLAND STICK INSECTS

5. Quoted in "Lord Howe Island Stick Insect," *San Diego Zoo Wildlife Alliance,* n.d. https://animals.sandiegozoo.org.

FOR FURTHER RESEARCH

BOOKS

Jaret C. Daniels, *Insects & Bugs for Kids*. Cambridge, MN: Adventure, 2021.

Susan H. Gray, *Monarch Butterfly Migration*. Ann Arbor, MI: Cherry Lake, 2021.

Martha London, *Pollinators: Animals Helping Plants Thrive*. Minneapolis, MN: Abdo, 2020.

INTERNET SOURCES

"Insect," *Britannica Kids*, n.d. https://kids.britannica.com.

Shay Maunz, "The Butterfly Problem," *Time for Kids*, April 7, 2021. www.timeforkids.com.

Allison Singer, "Monarch Butterflies and Other Animals That Migrate," *DK FindOut!*, May 9, 2016. www.dkfindout.com.

WEBSITES

Pollinator Partnership
www.pollinator.org

Founded in 1997, Pollinator Partnership works to provide people with information about the world's pollinators and resources to help conserve these important species. Its website provides information about rusty patched bumble bees, monarch butterflies, and more.

San Diego Zoo Wildlife Alliance: Arthropods
https://sandiegozoowildlifealliance.org/animals/arthropods

San Diego Zoo Wildlife Alliance is run by the San Diego Zoo in San Diego, California. The website contains information about many of the zoo's species as well as live video of its animals. The "Arthropods" page links to facts about the Lord Howe Island stick insect, monarch butterflies, and other endangered insects.

Zoos Victoria: Local Threatened Species
www.zoo.org.au/fighting-extinction/local-threatened-species

Zoos Victoria is a collection of zoos in Australia. Melbourne Zoo, part of Zoos Victoria, runs a Lord Howe Island stick insect breeding program. The Zoos Victoria "Local Threatened Species" page contains information about the Lord Howe Island stick insect as well as other endangered insects.

INDEX

antennae, 11, 46
Australia, 48, 55

Ball's Pyramid, 51, 52–54

Canada, 10, 13, 34
caterpillars, 13, 17
climate change, 9, 38–40
colonies, 6–8, 34–36, 38
conservationists, 17–19, 26–31, 43–45, 53–56

diets, 6, 8, 12, 13, 17, 22, 36, 40, 44, 50, 51, 56

eggs, 15, 17, 21, 27, 35–36, 49–50, 55
eyes, 6, 8, 12, 21, 35, 46

flowers, 7, 36, 38–40, 42, 44, 51

habitat loss, 6–8, 9, 16, 23–24, 38–39
heads, 11, 12, 32, 35
herbicides, 16–17, 18
hibernation, 15, 16, 34–36, 40, 44
Hine, James S., 23
Hine's emerald dragonflies, 20–31

invasive species, 24–26, 51, 52, 55–56

larvae, 21–22, 23, 26
life spans, 14, 22, 36

Lord Howe Island, 48–49, 51–52, 55–56
Lord Howe Island stick insects, 46–56

mates, 12, 15, 36, 51
migrations, 13–15, 19
monarch butterflies, 10–19

nectar, 6, 8, 12, 17, 18, 36, 44
nymphs, 49–50

pesticides, 24, 44
pollen, 6, 8, 36, 40–42, 44
pollinators, 18, 40–42, 43
pollution, 9, 24, 38
populations, 15–16, 23, 26, 40, 55
proboscis, 12

queen bees, 34–36, 39–40, 44

rusty-patched bumble bees, 6–8, 32–45

scales, 10–11
size, 20, 27, 46, 49

ultraviolet light, 8, 12
United States, 10, 13, 14, 23, 30, 34, 37, 39, 42

wings, 8, 10–11, 20, 27, 32, 34, 42
worker bees, 6–8, 35–36

62

IMAGE CREDITS

Cover: © Annette Shaff/Shutterstock Images
5: © bookguy/iStockphoto
7: © Sandrinka/Shutterstock Images
9: © tdlucas5000/Flickr
11: © Tom Koerner/US Fish and Wildlife Service
15: © Rafael Saldaña/Flickr
18: © Cathy Keifer/Shutterstock Images
21: © Richard & Susan Day/Danita Delimont/Alamy
25: © Ryan Hagerty/US Fish and Wildlife Service
29: © Danita Delimont/Shutterstock Images
31: © US Fish and Wildlife Service
33: © US Fish and Wildlife Service
37: © US Fish and Wildlife Service
39: © Red Line Editorial
41: © Taxomony/Shutterstock Images
43: © Digihelion/Shutterstock Images
45: © Lisa Nordstrom Kuck/US Fish and Wildlife Service
47: © Sandy Schletema/The AGE/Fairfax Media/Getty Images
48: © Emanuele Biggi/naturepl.com
53: © photosbyash/iStockphoto
57: © Danny Ye/Shutterstock Images

ABOUT THE AUTHOR

Christa Kelly is an author and editor from Minnesota. She lives with her wife, Clare, and their two cats, Casey and Honey Cheddar.